Tea for Three

*Hope you enjoy this book as much as I did writing it! God bless you and anyone who reads or listens to this book! May you learn to love the lessons contained here! Always be a **reader**! :)*

Your friend,
Greg Budzien
(Mr. Bud) :)

by Greg Budzien
Illustrated by Brigid Malloy

One time, Miss Ruby, in her best pink shawl,
And Miss Pearl, in her pretty pink pearls and all,
Sat down to enjoy a quaint pastry or three
With a cup, or two, of some fine green tea.

As Miss Pearl poured, as corgis like to do,
She said to Miss Ruby, "So, how are you?
Is there anything in your life that's new?"

Miss Ruby, with her shawl and her fancy French hat,
Pondered the question just there where she sat
And, after a miniature moment or two, said,
"Nothing too new, Pearl. How about you?"

"Well, it's strange you should ask the same question, my dear,
But indeed there is something you prob'ly should hear—
A rustling or bustling that came from my wall.
Now isn't that the strangest sound of all?"

Miss Ruby replied, "Wonder what it could be?"
Miss Pearl said, in turn, "Come on over and see."

So Miss Pearl and Miss Ruby, at a leisurely pace,
Had their cupcakes and tea as they sat in their place,
Since, when treats are at table, there's no need to race.

Eventually, off to Pearl's doghouse they went
To hear the strange sound—figure out what it meant.
When they got to her wall, leaning over they bent
And heard rustling or bustling right there near the vent...

"I think I know just what that sound is, dear Pearl.
I'm not really sure, but I'll give it a whirl.
That rustle you're hearing, without thinking twice,
I'm pretty sure means that your walls contain mice."

"MICE! YIKES!" exclaimed a now-startled Miss Pearl.
"That won't suffice!
I hear that they're dirty and not very nice!
They're all full of vice, and their children have lice!"

"Now, now," said Miss Ruby, "you've got to calm down.
Perhaps they're brand new to this part of our town.
We really don't know them, so just wait and see.
They're probably decent and nice as can be!"

But Pearl said, "Miss Ruby, you're being absurd.
When it comes to those mice-types, that's not what I've heard.
I've heard that, once here, many more mice will follow.
My walls will fill up and no longer be hollow.

It'll bring down the worth of our whole neighborhood.
Our schools will be ruined, and that can't be good.
Besides, I have heard they just can't get along.
Though I don't really know mice, my feelings are strong."

"Now Miss Pearl," Ruby said, "you must take my advice.
You have never once met nor known things about mice.
You must never pre-judge them, but give 'em a chance."
And she looked at Miss Pearl with a serious glance.

And just then, wouldn't you know it, through a hole in the wall
 Out came a mouse in a black and white shawl—
  All very pretty and nothing looked better,
   With threads intertwined and all woven together.

She said to Miss Pearl, and Miss Ruby as well,
 "Hello, my fine ladies!" as clear as a bell.
  "I hope that we three can stand still for a spell.
   I'm your new neighbor, and my friends call me Nell.

It's so nice to meet you; we've just moved in.
I hope that our doing so isn't a sin.
You've such a nice place, and it's filled with such charm.
I didn't think moving here'd cause any harm."

But Pearl said, "Not sure you belong here, my dear.
We're not used to your kind, and it's perfectly clear
That your fur doesn't match the type seen in this place.
It's much better for all if you give us some space."

Then the new-neighbor mouse said, as kind as can be,
   "But I'd rather be friends!" She spoke cordially.
      "And in time, our relationship's bound to grow strong,
         'Cause I've always thought, 'Can't we all get along?'"

Pearl said, "Your fur's darker, and ours is much lighter.
   See? Yours is much browner, and ours is much whiter.
      But I'm more a lover, and not much a fighter,
         So how can the three of us feel like we're tighter?"

Miss Nell said, "I'm thinking your thinking's quite dicey
When it comes to you thinking of things that are 'micey.'
When you lump us together, make us all of one stripe,
That's prejudice, and it makes us a stereotype.

And everyone knows that this judgment you show me
Is unfair because, really, you *really* don't know me.
So please judge us by worth, not the shade of our fur,
For to do otherwise would just make you a cur."

So, Miss Pearl gave her first thought another good think,
   And she soon changed her mind and then held up her drink.
      "Nell, I really do hear all the words that you've said,
         And it clears up the doubts and the dread in my head.

Let's toast to this moment where we all can agree
   That together is better, and it's plain to see,
      To do other than that is to cause a big fuss
         Over thoughts and behaviors that just aren't just!"

Then Miss Pearl looked at Nell, and she said with a smile,
"Would you like to sit down at my table awhile?
This is Miss Ruby, and I'm known as Miss P.
We were just getting ready to have some more tea!"

So the three of them sat down together at table
And they laughed and they talked as long as were able:
A bulldog, Miss Ruby; a corgi, Miss Pearl;
And Miss Nell, their new neighbor, all sipping Gray Earl!

Miss Ruby then cut them a cake filled with spice
And offered them both a most generous slice,
Saying, "Nothing I know of could be quite as nice
As a corgi and bulldog together with mice!"

Published by Orange Hat Publishing 2023
ISBN 9781645385530

Copyrighted © 2023 by Greg Budzien
All Rights Reserved
Tea for Three
Written by Greg Budzien
Illustrated by Brigid Malloy

This publication and all contents within may not be reproduced or transmitted in any part or in its entirety without the written permission of the author.

www.orangehatpublishing.com

Dedication

To my wife of thirty happy years, Kathy—the gentle, quiet, meek, and humble giver, who will always be my best friend and peerless Life companion. Love you and our Life together. I am forever blessed and grateful to have you, the MVP (most valuable person) in my world. Omnia ad majorem Dei gloriam. (*All for the greater glory of God*).

Acknowledgments

Thanks to my niece, Brigid Malloy, for her incomparable artwork as an illustrator, which inspired this book in the first place! You are so talented!! Much thanks to Sharon Ishizaki of Orange Hat Publishing. I admire her suggestions, encouragement, professionalism, guidance, and friendship throughout my first effort in the world of children's books. Thanks also to Jenna Zerbel for sharing her editing expertise. Most of all, thanks again to Kathy for her generous support, for allowing me to pursue and indulge in this project.

About the Author

Gregory J. Budzien was born August 20, 1955, in Milwaukee. He grew up in nearby Wauwatosa, where he attended Christ King Grade School and Wauwatosa West High School ('74). Greg then graduated summa cum laude from St. John's University in Collegeville, Minnesota ('78), with a major in English. After a year volunteering on the Jicarilla Apache Indian Reservation in New Mexico, Greg returned for a degree in English Education at the University of Wisconsin-Milwaukee, eventually earning a Masters in Education [Professional Development] from the University of Wisconsin-Whitewater. Greg taught AP English and other English classes for twenty-eight years at Arrowhead High School, where he also coached girls cross-country, freshman boys basketball, and girls and boys golf. Greg currently lives in easy, retired circumstances with his loving wife, Kathy, in wonderful Chenequa, Wisconsin.

CPSIA information can be obtained
at www.ICGtesting.com
Printed in the USA
BVRC090343090223
658165BV00002B/3